BUGATTI VEYRON

By Megan Ray Durkin

Kaleidoscope
Minneapolis, MN

The Quest for Discovery Never Ends

This edition is co-published by agreement between Kaleidoscope and World Book, Inc.

Kaleidoscope Publishing, Inc.
6012 Blue Circle Drive
Minnetonka, MN 55343 U.S.A.

World Book, Inc.
180 North LaSalle St., Suite 900
Chicago IL 60601 U.S.A.

Kaleidoscope ISBNs
978-1-64519-025-7 (library bound)
978-1-64494-232-1 (paperback)
978-1-64519-125-4 (ebook)

World Book ISBN
978-0-7166-4326-5 (library bound)

Library of Congress Control Number
2019940216

Printed in the United States of America.

Bigfoot lurks within one of the images in this book. It's up to you to find him!

TABLE OF CONTENTS

CHAPTER 1

The Super Sport was a lighter, faster version of the Bugatti Veyron.

WORLD'S FASTEST CAR

The day was just right for the ultimate test. The sun shone down. The air was clear. And the track was dry. It was July 2010. Engineers gathered at a high-speed test track. It was a Volkswagen track in Germany. Pierre-Henri Raphanel was the driver. He was testing the Bugatti Veyron Super Sport. He put on his helmet. He fastened his gloves. He pulled the safety belts tight. Engineers checked the car one last time.

The spoiler extends to help the car go faster.

The Super Sport was orange and black. Its powerful engine purred. Three, two, one, go! The Veyron took off. Raphanel reached 62 miles per hour (100 km/h). It took just 2.5 seconds. The **turbocharged** W16 engine gave him 1,200 **horsepower**. The Veyron roared like a jet. The scene out the windows was a blur. Raphanel sped down the track.

FUN FACT
The Veyron can cover a football field in one second at top speed.

The car reached 140 miles per hour (225 km/h). Then **hydraulics** lowered the car. A rear wing and **spoiler** extended. These **aerodynamic** features kept the car on the track. Special tires hugged the track. The car went faster and faster. Soon Raphanel reached top speed. He reached 267.856 miles per hour (431.072 km/h). Then the rear wing flapped up. Raphanel brought the car to a stop. Stopping took only ten seconds.

PARTS OF A BUGATTI VERYON

FUN FACT
The Veyron can run out of gas in twelve minutes.

Guinness World Records was there. The Super Sport broke a record. Guinness named it the world's fastest **production car**. The Bugatti team proved themselves. Their Veyron was a true winner.

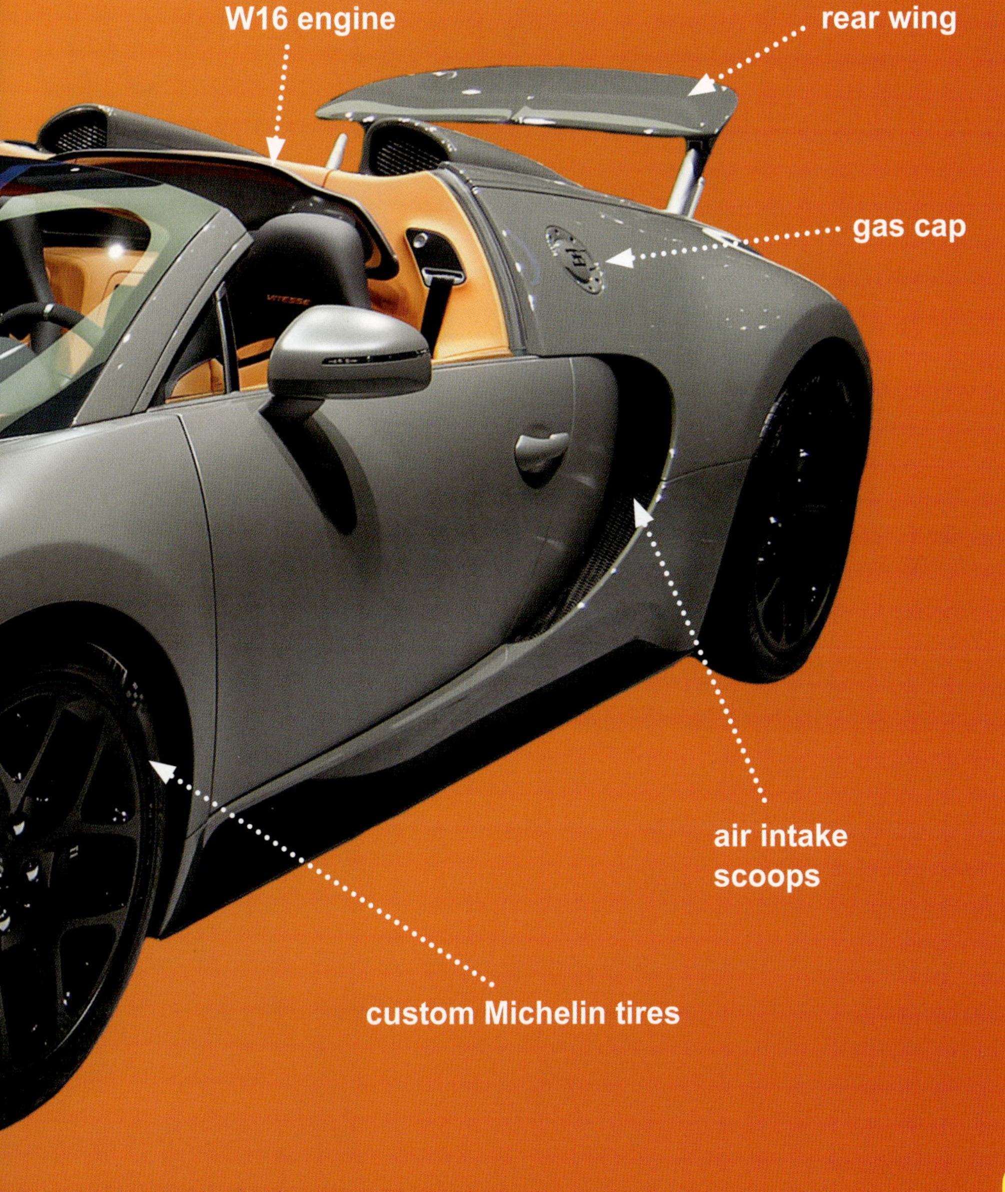

CHAPTER 2

THE FACTORY

Manny loved the Bugatti Veyron. He read about it in *Guinness World Records*. His biggest dream was coming true. His family was taking a trip to Molsheim, France. Manny would get to tour the Bugatti factory!

Manny's family arrived. They admired the beautiful building. The factory has been there since 1909. That's when the company started. A tour was ready to go. Manny's family walked into a modern building. Bugatti called it the *Atelier*. Atelier is the French word for an artist's workshop.

Bugatti's headquarters have been at Château St. Jean since 1909.

THE SUNKEN BUGATTI

A 1925 Bugatti car became famous. It spent seventy-five years in a lake. The owner couldn't pay the import tax. The car wasn't worth much. The police rolled it into the lake. That was in 1934. A diving club rescued it in 2009. They sold it for charity. It sold for $368,600!

The guide told them the history of Bugatti. The founder was Ettore Bugatti. His dream was to make special cars. Bugatti's cars combined power and art. This craftmanship is still part of the company.

Volkswagen is a German car company. It bought Bugatti in 1998. Its goal was to build the world's fastest production car. The Veyron achieved that goal. Volkswagen built 450 Veyrons. There were different models of the Veyron. The Veyron Super Sport set the world record. Only thirty of them were made.

Ettore Bugatti saw a car as a work of art.

FUN FACT

The letters EB, for Ettore Bugatti, are on the grille of every Bugatti car.

The Veyrons were built at the same property where Ettore Bugatti built his race cars.

FUN FACT
It took five weeks to build each Veyron.

Inside the factory, Manny was amazed. Everything was assembled by hand. Some workers wore white gloves. The car's owner selected the paint colors. The interior was made from fine leather. Each Veyron was truly a work of art. Ettore Bugatti would have been proud. Manny was happy to see it all. He now knew what it took to build these amazing cars. It made Manny love the Veyron even more.

Where the Bugatti Veyron Was Made

1 Molsheim, France: Bugatti headquarters; The Atelier, where the Veyron was assembled

2 Salzgitter, Germany: The Volkswagen Engine Factory, where the Veyron's engines were built

CHAPTER 3

SUPER SHOW

It was the 2015 Geneva International Motor Show. The Veyrons were the stars. The last Bugatti Veyron was on display. It was the 450th Veyron. The designers named it La Finale. It meant the final one.

The doors opened. The Veyrons were in the center. Everyone was excited to see their favorite **supercar**.

The Veyron had won many awards. It was once called the car of the decade.

The first Veyron ever produced was parked at the front. It was red and blue. It was made in 2005. Across the aisle was La Finale. It was burgundy and black. The exterior was made of smooth **carbon fiber**. This made the car lighter. A lighter car was a faster car.

The Bugatti Veyron La Finale was one of a kind.

THE VEYRON GRAND SPORT VITESSE

IN DETAIL

COST: $2.3 MILLION

Length: 14.6 feet (4.5 m)

Weight: 4,400 pounds (1,996 kg)

Top Speed: 255 miles per hour (410 km/h)

Time from 0–62 miles per hour (0–100 km/h): 2.6 seconds

The Veyron's W16 engine is at the back of the car.

A Veyron engine was on display. A show guide described it to visitors. She explained that many cars have V8 engines. This name comes from the engine's shape. But the Veyron is different. It has a W16 engine. A W16 is two V8 engines stuck together. That's a lot of horsepower. It could get very hot. That's why the Veyron had ten **radiators**. It also had air scoops on top of the car. They sucked in extra air. The air fed the engine. The Veyron had lots of power. But it was very smooth and safe.

The car show was getting crowded. Lots of people wanted to see the Veyrons. The show guide was talking to a group. She told them that Volkswagen produced the Veyron for ten years. There were different models in that time. The original was the Bugatti Veyron 16.4. Then came the Grand Sport. Next came the Super Sport. The last one was the Grand Sport Vitesse. There were also special editions of the car. She told them that La Finale had already been sold. A customer bought it for $2.6 million.

The one-of-a-kind L'Or Blanc was one of many Veyron special editions.

SPECIAL EDITION VEYRONS

There were many special editions of the Veyron. One was L'Or Blanc. This car had porcelain accents. It was one of a kind. Another was the Bernar Venet. Venet is a famous French artist. He designed the car. He included math formulas in the design. These cars honored Ettore Bugatti. They were works of art.

CHAPTER 4

THE LUCKY ONES

The Veyron is completely sold out. But its legacy lives on. Volkswagen first announced the Veyron in 1999. People said it was impossible. Few people believed a car could go that fast. Engineers had to create new parts. But the Veyron exceeded expectations. The Super Sport is still one of the fastest cars. It proved an important point. Cars could go fast and still be stylish.

The Bugatti Veyron was a record-breaking car.

Veyron owners could customize the colors of the interior and exterior of the car.

Bugatti is a symbol of wealth and luxury. The Veyron is an expensive car. An oil change costs over $20,000. A Veyron is more expensive to operate than a private jet. It is a car for the rich and famous. Only a few people in the world can own one. But everyone can be a Veyron fan.

FAME AND FORTUNE

Many celebrities own Bugatti Veyrons. Hip-hop artist Jay-Z got a Veyron for his birthday. Actor Tom Cruise drove a Veyron to a movie premiere. Sports stars Tom Brady and Cristiano Ronaldo own Veyrons.

Bugatti continues to develop impressive cars. Bugatti revealed a new car in 2016. It was called the Chiron. Five hundred Chirons will be made. Buyers come to Molsheim. They customize the car. Bugatti's other car is the Divo. Only forty were made. Not just anyone could buy one.

Divo buyers had to already own a Chiron. Each Divo cost over $5 million. All forty sold out in one day. Bugatti will continue to grow. But it was the Veyron that made Bugatti famous.

The Bugatti Chiron replaced the Veyron.

BEYOND THE BOOK

After reading the book, it's time to think about what you learned. Try the following exercises to jumpstart your ideas.

THINK

THAT'S NEWS TO ME. The Veyron Super Sport set the world record for fastest production car in 2010. How might news sources be able to fill in more detail about this? What new information could you find in news articles? Where could you go to find those sources?

CREATE

PRIMARY SOURCES. A primary source is an original document, photograph, or interview. Make a list of primary sources you might be able to find about the Veyron. What new information might you learn from these sources?

SHARE

WHAT'S YOUR OPINION? Ettore Bugatti saw his cars as works of art. Do you agree that a car can be a work of art? Do you disagree? Use evidence from the text to support your answer. Share your position and evidence with a friend. Does your friend agree with you?

GROW

REAL-LIFE RESEARCH. What places could you visit to learn more about the Veyron? What other things could you learn while you were there?

Visit www.ninjaresearcher.com/0257 to learn how to take your research skills and book report writing to the next level!

SEARCH LIKE A PRO
Learn about how to use search engines to find useful websites.

FACT OR FAKE?
Discover how you can tell a trusted website from an untrustworthy resource.

TEXT DETECTIVE
Explore how to zero in on the information you need most.

SHOW YOUR WORK
Research responsibly—learn how to cite sources.

WRITE

GET TO THE POINT
Learn how to express your main ideas.

PLAN OF ATTACK
Learn prewriting exercises and create an outline.

DOWNLOADABLE REPORT FORMS

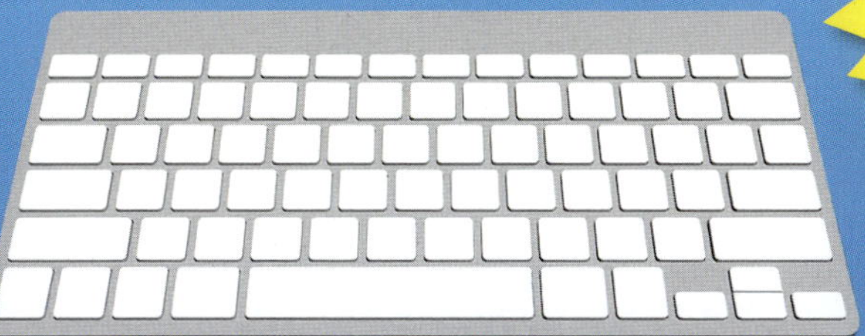

FURTHER RESOURCES

BOOKS

Cruz, Calvin. *Bugatti Veyron*. Bellwether Media, 2016.

Doeden, Matt. *Sports Cars*. Capstone Press, 2019.

Oachs, Emily Rose. *Bugatti Chiron.* Bellwether Media, 2018.

WEBSITES

FACTSURFER

Factsurfer.com gives you a safe, fun way to find more information.

1. Go to www.factsurfer.com.
2. Enter "Bugatti Veyron" into the search box and click 🔍.
3. Select your book cover to see a list of related websites.

GLOSSARY

aerodynamic: An aerodynamic design reduces the drag, or pull, on a car as it moves through air. The Veyron's aerodynamic design helped it reach very high speeds.

carbon fiber: Carbon fiber is a very strong, lightweight material. Using carbon fiber to build a car makes it lighter and faster.

horsepower: One horsepower is the power it takes to lift 550 pounds one foot in one second. The Veyron engines all had more than 1,000 horsepower.

hydraulics: Hydraulics is a system that uses fluid to move parts. The Veyron used hydraulics in many of its systems.

production car: A production car is one produced for sale to the public. Someone could buy a production car, like a Veyron, and drive it on the street. It is also called a street legal car.

radiators: Radiators are devices used to keep the engine of a vehicle from getting too hot. The Veyron had ten radiators.

spoiler: A spoiler is a fin or wing that changes the airflow around the car. The Veyron had a large spoiler in the back to help steer and stop the car.

supercar: A supercar is a very expensive, fast, or powerful car. The Veyron was the top supercar of its time.

turbocharged: A turbocharged car uses blowers called turbochargers to give more power to the engine. All Veyrons had turbocharged engines.

INDEX

PHOTO CREDITS

The images in this book are reproduced through the courtesy of: Max Earey/Shutterstock Images, front cover (car), pp. 4–5, 6–7; sumroeng chinnapan/Shutterstock Images, front cover (sky); Art Konovalov/Shutterstock Images, p. 3; Massimo Campanari/Shutterstock Images, p. 4; Neil Balderson/Shutterstock Images, pp. 8–9; Parmigiani Fleurier/PPR/AP Images, pp. 10–11; VanderWolf Images/Shutterstock Images, pp. 12–13, 19; Lpettet/iStockphoto, p. 13; Christian Lutz/AP Images, p. 14; Red Line Editorial, p. 15; Zavatskiy Aleksandr/Shutterstock Images, pp. 16–17; Dong liu/Shutterstock Images, p. 18; Cottin Lucille/Shutterstock Images, pp. 20–21; Sjo/iStockphoto, pp. 22–23; jangeltun/iStockphoto, p. 23; Gustavo Fadel/Shutterstock Images, pp. 24–25; Kaukola Photography/Shutterstock Images, pp. 26–27; EvrenKalinbacak/Shutterstock Images, p. 30.

ABOUT THE AUTHOR

Megan Ray Durkin has been a teacher for many years. She loves to share her enthusiasm for books with children everywhere.